Beetle and Bug had been |
   nowhere at all
For a while when, clearing a
   drawer in the hall,
Beetle discovered some guide-
   books and maps —
Old ones, in parchment, with fold-
   outs and flaps.

3

"This is Egypt," he breathed with
  excitement and glee,
"Where a long time ago there
  were beetles like me

4

Who were worshipped as sacred
and treated as kings,
Who were buried in tombs with
their favourite things."

"Then why don't we go
   there," said Bug, "for a look
As the tombs are still standing, it
   says in this book?

And while we're about it, enjoy a
   nice cruise,
On Rug, down this river that's
   marked here in blues."

So they unrolled their flyer and
   boarded and flew
South-east to Egypt, the way that
   Rug knew,

Though once they'd come down
  on the Nile river delta,
They started to sweat and they
  started to swelter.

"This Egypt," said Bug, "is a hot
  desert land,
Made almost entirely of baked
  mud and sand.

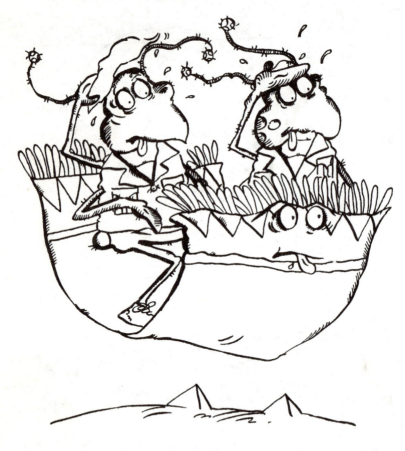

10

We must get ourselves sun hats, a canopy, shades,

Swimming trunks, sandals, some buckets and spades."

So they asked Rug to stop at the
nearest bazaar,
And they bought their supplies
and a handmade guitar

12

Which they couldn't resist, plus
some good cotton cloth

And a small statuette of the old
moon god, Thoth.

Then just as they thought they
    might start on their cruise,
A toothless old beggar in rags and
    no shoes
Tugged at their elbows and
    wheedled and whined,

"I show where the great Scarab
  Pharaoh's enshrined . . .
I take you tomorrow, I take you
  today,
For me, old Habbibi, alone knows
  the way . . ."

"Oh, Beetle," said Bug, "that tomb
   is renowned.
Though many have tried, it has
   never been found.

Imagine if we ... *did* ... discover
the site ...
Our names would be famous," he
said, "overnight."

So they told old Habbibi they'd
    leave then and there,
And agreed on a fee for his time
    and the fare,

And they followed behind
  through the dust and the heat,
As he sped through the crowds —
  up alley, down street.

Till they got to the docks and the
old beggar's boat,

Which was so full of holes it
seemed hardly to float.

But Habbibi kept smiling his wide
   toadying smile,
Which he smiled all that night as
   they sailed down the Nile.

21

Though when daybreak came, it
  was gone from his face
And a bad-tempered snarl had
  arrived in its place.

"You take all your things!" he spat
  with a frown,
As he tied up the boat at the ghost
  of a town.

Then pushing and shoving, he
rushed them ashore,

And frogmarched them on
through a worn-away door,

And forced them up steps to a
worn-away room,

Where he left them alone to fret in
the gloom.

"I think," muttered Beetle, "we're
    in a slight jam,
Or even the victims of some sort
    of scam.

That Habbibi's no guide — he's a
 villain, a hood.
He has no tomb to show us, he's
 up to no good!"

And as if to confirm it, loud
    laughter was heard,
With the clinking and clanking of
    boots that were spurred,

And swinging their swords and
  hitching their pants,

Into the room burst a gang of Red
  Ants . . .

"Ha, ha!" roared the leader. "My
name is Rob Graves,
And that's what I do with my
comrades, these knaves.

Though plundering tombs isn't all
    that we do
. . . We also rob tourists. We're
    going to rob you!"

"We've nothing of value," quaked
    Beetle, "to take."
"And that statue's not real,"
    quivered Bug, "it's a fake."

But Graves had lost interest in
   Beetle and Bug
And their statue of Thoth — his
   eyes were on Rug!

"Nothing of value?" he roared
    and he jeered,
As his comrades rubbed hands
    and bellowed and cheered.

"My spies in the city would
    contradict that.
They report you came in on a
    magical mat.

A mat that can fly and can sail
  and dry-ski,
Which in my line of work is the
  carpet for me!"

Then to their dismay, right in front
    of their eyes,
That robber, Rob Graves, took
    their Rug as his prize.

While two of his mates, tattooed
  top to toe,
Said, "OK, you lice, on your feet.
  Now let's go . . ."

And frogmarched them off, while
whistling old tunes,

Through mile after mile after mile
of hot dunes.

Till they came to a valley — the
    hottest by far —
Where the robbers said, "So, you
    great nits, here we are . . .

In the valley of tombs that the
   Scarabs once cursed,
Where all who set foot die of
   sunstroke and thirst!"

"Oh, Beetle," said Bug, as the
    robbers departed.
"What a terrible fate, though I'm
    more broken-hearted
At the thought of our Rug at the
    mercy of Graves
And his villainous whims and his
    murderous knaves!"

"Oh, Rug will survive," said
    Beetle, " and, Bug,
It's us you should cry for — our
    lives down the plug.
And all for the sake of some old
    mausoleum
And wanting our names in the
    British Museum."

43

"Well, let's not waste breath or the
  little we've left
Regretting what's happened," said
  Bug, "or the theft.

And though this is hardly the
  journey we planned,
To get out of the sun we must dig
  in the sand . . ."

So they started to burrow and
they started to bore,

To scrape and to scratch and to
burrow some more,

When quite unexpectedly Beetle
  called out,
"I've hit something hard, so
  what's *this* about?"

And Bug scurried over and Beetle
dug deep,

And uncovered some steps that
were narrow and steep,

Which led to a door that was
locked up and sealed,

But they crawled through a crack
. . . What a sight was revealed!

There were statues and vases and
glittering gold,

There were ebony, ivory, treasures
untold,

There were game-boards and
chariots and four-poster beds,

And incredible carvings of ancient
gods' heads.

"Oh boy!" whispered Bug. "What
a place to take off in,
And look over here, there's a solid
gold coffin!"
And hearts beating wildly, they
prised up the lid

And found themselves facing a
   head that was hid
By a gold and jewelled mask
   making everything clear —
The great Scarab Pharaoh was
   mummified here!

And such was their reverence at
  what they'd uncovered,
At what, through misfortune and
  chance, they'd discovered,

That they fell to their knees and
  said a short prayer.
*"If you'll help us get home, then, O
  Scarab, we swear*

We will leave you in peace, we will
   not tell a mite,
That we know where your soul comes
   to play of a night."

Then almost at once came a
   sudden cold blast
Of fresh evening air — and their
   ordeal was past.

"You escaped and you found us,
you sweetheart!" cried Bug,
As into the tomb swept their
brave magic Rug!

And when they'd resealed and re-
  covered the tomb,
As they'd promised they would if
  they did escape doom,

Rug sped them away from the hot
to the cool,
Though swooping down first to
show them the pool

Where somehow Rob Graves and
    his villainous jocks
Had been tipped, by the excellent
    Rug, to the crocs.

And as they observed those
    knaves disappearing,
They saw old Habbibi on deck —
    he was cheering.

"I'm free of those bandits, I'm out
 of their pay!"
And Bug said to Beetle, "Well,
 what a great day!"

Then they stretched out on Rug,
sighing "Rug, you're the
best . . ."
And flew home to bed — for a
well-deserved rest.